Five reasons why you'll love this book:

Ideal for animal lovers

Full of Christmassy magic

Beautiful illustrations that will really get you in the festive spirit

Lucy helps a poorly rabbit

Make a wish!

Here's a taste of the magic to come . . .

'Lucy—what's this?' asked Dad. 'I found it under your pillow.' He gave Lucy a little red cloth pouch as he took the folded-up bed out to the garage.

Lucy had never seen the red pouch before. It was as red as Father Christmas's coat, and it sparkled as Lucy held it. It was so beautiful, embroidered with a picture of Father Christmas and a little white Christmas reindeer. Lucy opened the pouch, and inside was glittering, magical dust—all the colours of the rainbow, just like the stars she had seen in the globe. Folded up small and covered in glitter was a note. Lucy felt her heart beating fast. Her fingers were tingling the way they had felt when she had wished

on the snow globe—something magical was

happening, she was sure of it. She opened the

note and read:

To Lucy.

This magic dust is especially for you
For with your kind heart you will
know what to do.
So sprinkle it carefully down from
above
On those who are lost and need
friendship and love
And magic will happen for them
and for you
And your christmas wishes
will then all come true.

To my dear friends Katy, Simon,
Lizzie, and Esther Burder

OXFORD
UNIVERSITY PRESS

Great Clarendon Street, Oxford OX2 6DP
Oxford University Press is a department of the University of Oxford.
It furthers the University's objective of excellence in research, scholarship,
and education by publishing worldwide. Oxford is a registered trade mark of
Oxford University Press in the UK and in certain other countries

British Library Cataloguing in Publication Data
Data available
ISBN: 978-0-19-274331-2

1 3 5 7 9 10 8 6 4 2

Printed in Great Britain
Paper used in the production of this book is a natural,
recyclable product made from wood grown in sustainable forests.
The manufacturing process conforms to the environmental
regulations of the country of origin.

LUCY'S MAGIC
SNOW GLOBE

Anne Booth

OXFORD
UNIVERSITY PRESS

Chapter One

21st December

It was Christmas time and Lucy's home was full of delicious baking smells, fairy lights, and decorations. It was especially busy in Lucy's house this year because her dad's friends from Australia were coming to stay with them for Christmas.

They were supposed to be moving in to a house in the village, but their new home wouldn't be ready until the New Year.

Lucy was in her bedroom with her little cat Merry, her pyjama-case dog Scruffy, and her rocking horse, Rocky.

She was sitting cross-legged on her bed, shaking her snow globe. She loved the snow globe. It lit up at night and there was a pretty Christmassy woodland scene inside. Once, she had even thought she'd seen Father Christmas and a reindeer. It normally cheered her up to watch the pretty white and silver flakes falling, but today she sighed.

'Christmas was going to be really special this year. Gran was coming to stay in my room after her shoulder operation and now it's all changed. It was going to be like a fun sleepover with Gran, but now Mum says I have to sleep downstairs with this girl called Sita . . .' said Lucy to her three friends. 'I've never even met her and I've got to share a room with her just because she's the same age as me. What if she doesn't like animals? What if she doesn't like naughty cats like you, Merry?'

Lucy put the snow globe carefully back on her windowsill and rolled a pen across the room for Merry, who jumped on it delightedly. She never tired of that game.

'Lucy? Have you cleared your bedroom yet?' called Mum up the stairs. Lucy looked at the floor. It had been fine before Merry had padded upstairs to pay her a visit. First Merry had jumped on the wastepaper basket and tipped all the rubbish out. She had looked so sweet patting all the scrunched-up paper and chasing old pens that Lucy had forgotten that she was supposed to be getting her room ready for Gran. Then Merry had jumped up on the chest of drawers and knocked a pot of glitter all over Lucy's bedroom carpet.

'Oh, Merry! You really are a Christmas cat now!' Lucy had laughed, as Merry left little glittery paw prints all over the room. 'It's a good thing I've made all the Christmas cards already.'

This year Lucy had made lots of Christmas cards and drawn a picture of a special magic baby reindeer on the front of each, so she had needed lots of glitter. She had sold them on a stall at school to raise money for her gran's Wildlife Rescue Centre. Then she gave the money and a special card on which she had written 'Get Well Soon' to Gran in the hospital. Gran had put it beside her hospital bed.

'Oh, Lucy!' Gran had said. 'This is definitely the nicest card in the ward! What a kind girl you are! I can't wait until Christmas. We'll have a special girls' sleepover, you and me, and talk about what we'll do when the Wildlife Rescue Centre opens again. At least whilst I'm in hospital I can make the Centre better. I'm getting so much building work done and it would have been too noisy for the sick animals if they'd been there. We're having a bigger kitchen with new sinks and cupboards, and a little quiet area, and even a new aviary at the back. There are going to be heated cages and a place for bigger animals in the garden too. It'll be wonderful. So it's all worked out very well, and we're so lucky that Meadowbank Sanctuary took the little hedgehogs and the robin.'

It was really exciting but Lucy missed Gran and helping out at the Centre very much. But she was glad that the operation was over and that Gran was coming to stay for a few weeks. Lucy had planned to spend their sleepover time every day talking about how they would look after the hedgehogs and deer and foxes and owls and other birds and animals when the Centre opened again. Lucy loved animals so much.

'Oh, Lucy!' Mum was in the doorway looking hot and bothered. She was holding one end of a camp bed she had got out of the attic, and Oscar, Lucy's big brother, who was in his first year at secondary school, was holding the other. 'This room was supposed to be ready by now. Honestly, Lucy—what a mess!'

'I'm sorry, Mum,' said Lucy, trying to ignore the pretend-shocked face Oscar was pulling behind Mum's back. He could be so annoying. And he didn't even have to move out of his bedroom. It wasn't fair. 'It was ready but Merry tipped the wastepaper basket over.'

'Well, she'll have to go downstairs in her basket for now. I'm not even sure if she should sleep on your bed in the kitchen whilst our visitors are here, Lucy,' said Mum. 'Go downstairs and put her in the sitting room and then come back up and sort out this room with me.'

Lucy scooped Merry up from the floor into her arms. Even though Mum was cross, she couldn't help smiling at the naughty little cat. Ever since she had arrived in their home as a little Christmas kitten, the whole family loved her, but Lucy loved her most of all, and one of her favourite things in

the world was going to sleep with Merry
curled up beside Scruffy, her pyjama-
case dog, with Rocky the rocking horse
looking on with his kind, patient eyes.

Mum and Oscar opened out the
camp bed in Lucy's room for Lucy's
sleepover night with Gran. When the
visitors arrived, both girls would sleep

on camp beds in the kitchen, and Dad and Mum were going to be sleeping in the lounge and giving their bed to Sita's parents. 'It's not fair if you can't sleep on my bed just because that girl is coming,' grumbled Lucy to Merry as she put her down in her basket in the sitting room. Merry was perfectly happy there and curled up to go to sleep, but Lucy still felt cross as she went back upstairs. The house was full of sparkly decorations and the Christmas tree was up, but Lucy didn't feel Christmassy any more at all.

'Why do we have to have visitors?' she muttered as she tidied up.

'I think we're going to have to put Rocky in the garage over Christmas,' said Mum, looking around Lucy's room. 'Some of the luggage from Australia can go in Oscar's room, but we'll have to store some in your room too. Gran says she doesn't mind.'

'No! It's not fair!' said Lucy, shocked. 'Poor Rocky! He hasn't done anything wrong. He'll want to stay with Gran or me. He'll be so lonely in the garage. Please, Mum—don't put him there!'

'Oh, Lucy,' sighed Mum. She called Oscar into Lucy's room. 'Look—why don't you two go out to the park? I'll try to sort the rooms out and make things fit.'

'Do I have to take Lucy with me?' complained Oscar. 'My friends will probably be there having a kick-around, and she'll just get in the way.'

'Yes, you do,' said Mum. 'You both need some fresh air and I need some

14

space. Take your phone, Oscar.'

The weather was very cold and damp, and Oscar and Lucy both put their coats on very grumpily.

'Hurry up, Lucy!' Oscar said, and ran ahead. Lucy had to run her fastest to catch up with him.

'Hi, Will!' Oscar shouted when he saw his friends. He rushed over to them.

Lucy felt cross and tired and left out. She didn't feel like playing on the slide and the swings on her own. She would much rather have been at home with Merry and Rocky and Scruffy. She sat on the bench and thought about her best school friend.

'I can't even visit Rosie because her family have gone to her Grandad's for Christmas,' she sighed.

Lucy got up and walked around the edge of the football pitch. Suddenly, she noticed something moving in the hedge. She bent down and moved the branches to one side and there, on the cold ground, was a tiny baby rabbit, all alone and with a nasty cut on his leg. He was very sweet but Lucy knew he was also very poorly. He didn't try to run away when he saw her. Instead, he just lay there with his ears back, looking frightened.

'Oh, please don't be scared,' whispered Lucy. She knew from her work with her

gran that you shouldn't normally
touch a wild animal, but she could
see that this little rabbit was injured.

She looked around but there was no sign of rabbit holes or any warren for it to shelter in, just a flat football pitch beside a road. He wouldn't survive on his own. He really needed her help.

Chapter Two

'Oscar!' Lucy called, but he was busy with his friends.

'Over here, Sam!' Oscar shouted, as he ran to receive the ball.

'Oscar!' Lucy yelled again, but it was no use. Lucy summoned up all her courage and ran onto the field to get him.

'Hey, Oscar! Your sister's on the pitch!' the other footballers complained. Lucy wanted to run off, but she knew the baby rabbit was depending on her to get help.

'What are you doing?' Oscar said, annoyed, as he ran over.

'Oscar—look what I've found in the bushes. It's a little rabbit and he's hurt,' said Lucy, leading Oscar to the hedge. Oscar's best friends Will and Fergus left the others and came over to see.

'Where has he come from?' said Oscar, kneeling down.

'I don't know but we can't leave him here. He won't survive now he's hurt. I'm going to have to bring him home. He needs to be kept warm,' said Lucy, unzipping her coat.

'You can have my old jumper if you like—I was using it as one of the goalposts,' said Fergus, and he ran to get it.

Lucy gently placed Fergus's jumper over the rabbit and scooped it up so that the rabbit was cosy and securely wrapped, and couldn't kick. Then she carried it inside her coat. She could feel his heart thumping against her chest.

'Don't worry, little rabbit,' she whispered to it. 'I'll be your friend. I will look after you.'

Oscar, Will, and Fergus walked back with Lucy, past the houses with all the Christmas decorations in their gardens and windows. Will and Fergus didn't normally talk to her. It felt good being in a group of friends for a little while, even if they were big boys.

'Will your sister be able to help it?' she heard Will ask Oscar.

'Yeah—she does lots with my gran so she knows loads about animals. She'll be able to make it better,' said Oscar confidently.

Lucy felt really proud. Oscar didn't often say nice things about her. Most of the time he was too busy at school or playing football or drums to really notice her. She didn't mind too much as she was mostly with Gran, helping out at the Centre, or playing with Merry, or visiting Rosie in the next village, but it felt good to hear him say that to his friends. Maybe they would talk to her more now.

'Mum—Lucy's back with a rabbit!' called Oscar up the stairs when they got back. 'Fergus and Will and I are going back down the park. Bye!' and the boys banged the door behind them and ran off back to their game, leaving Lucy on her own in the hallway, holding her warm bundle.

'Lucy?' said Mum, coming out on to the landing. 'What's that you've got?'

'It's a little rabbit, Mum. It was injured and I couldn't leave it under the hedge alone,' said Lucy.

'Oh, dear,' Mum sighed, her arms full of sheets. 'What are we going to do? I suppose we could take it to the big wildlife sanctuary, but that means a two-hour round trip, and I've got so much to do. Is it very badly hurt?'

'I'm not sure. He has a cut on his leg, and he's so small and away from his warren. He won't survive on his own. Can't I look after him—please?' pleaded Lucy. 'I've helped Gran with baby rabbits before. I know where she keeps her special baby rabbit food.'

Just then they heard the key in the lock and Dad came in, looking very cheerful and wearing some tinsel around his head.

'I'm on holiday—hooray! Christmas starts NOW!' he said, and went to give Lucy a hug.

'No, Dad—I've got a baby rabbit in my coat,' said Lucy.

'Have you, indeed?' said Dad. 'Can I have a look?'

Mum came down the stairs and they all peeped in. The tiny rabbit's eyes were closed, and it was breathing very fast.

'He's very sweet, but he looks poorly, Lucy,' said Mum.

'I don't think we should drive it miles away to the wildlife sanctuary. I think it needs peace and quiet to get better,' said Lucy. 'Please, Dad— please can we get one of Gran's cages and the baby rabbit food and bring it here tonight? I do know what to do, honestly.'

Dad looked at Mum.

'Just for tonight, Lucy,' said Mum.

'Your dad or I will have to take it to the wildlife sanctuary tomorrow as we just won't have room when our visitors come.'

Lucy opened her mouth to argue but her dad gave her a wink.

'Come on Lucy Lu—pop the little fellow in Merry's cat basket for five minutes and we'll drive to Gran's quickly and collect the stuff you need.'

Merry rushed out into the hallway as if she heard her name.

'Now, Merry, we're borrowing your cat carrier,' said Lucy. 'This baby rabbit is called a kitten, like you were, and he needs quiet, like Gran does, to get better.' Lucy got the wicker cat carrier from the hall cupboard and moved some Christmas cards to the side to make room for it on the hall table. Lucy carefully laid the little rabbit in Fergus's old jumper inside the carrier and closed the door. Then she picked up Merry and gave her a quick cuddle and kiss on the top of her head. The little cat purred and didn't want to be put down.

'I'm sorry, Merry, but I'm going to lock you in the kitchen. I don't trust you not to bother the kitten,' said Lucy. Merry gave an indignant mew and they could hear her scratching at the door as they left.

'Your gran will be very proud of you,' said Lucy's dad in Gran's house. They packed some rabbit food and some hay in a cage, ready to bring home. 'But Lucy, I think your Mum is right—I'm not sure we can look after it over Christmas with all our visitors here too.'

'I wish they weren't coming,' said Lucy. 'There isn't enough room, and they are just making things difficult.'

'Don't say that, Lucy,' said Dad. 'I want you to make Sita, and her dad and mum welcome. It's not easy for them being away from the rest of their family at Christmas. They need friends.'

'Why did they come then?' said Lucy.

'Sita's dad, Prajit, is coming to work here for a year. Sita is going to your school, so that's why I want you to be friends. It'll be too busy at our house for you to look after this little chap— you'll need to take care of Sita.'

'I'd rather look after the rabbit,' said Lucy.

'I'm sure that's true, Lucy,' said Dad, smiling, 'but poor Sita needs a friend too!'

When they got home, Lucy rushed to the hall table and looked inside the carrier to see how the rabbit was. He was very weak when they took him out of Merry's cat basket, and he didn't try

to struggle whilst Dad helped to hold him and Lucy bathed his leg as Gran had taught her. Then they transferred him to the cage. Oscar came back from football and they all sat down to dinner. Merry crept in and sat on Lucy's feet like an extra furry slipper.

The phone rang just as they were clearing the table. Mum went to answer it and came back smiling.

'Well, it's good news from the hospital. They say Gran can leave the ward and we can go and collect her straight away,' she said.

'Hooray!' said Lucy. 'I can ask her about the rabbit.'

'I just don't know how we are going to fit everyone in!' said Mum to Dad.

'We'll manage!' said Dad, giving her a hug. 'Come on, Lucy—let's go and get her now!'

Chapter Three

'Well done, Lucy!' said Gran. She gave the little rabbit a very quick examination. 'You've done just the right thing. It's a little male rabbit. He would never have managed on his own with a hurt paw like that.'

'Couldn't we just find a rabbit burrow and leave him there?' said Oscar.

'No, I'm afraid that would be very dangerous. You can't put a wild rabbit down any old burrow. We don't know where he comes from, and the rabbits already in the burrow might think he was an enemy and fight him. He would have no warren to live in and have to live above ground on his own—and that isn't safe. He's not ready to go anywhere yet anyway—he is far too weak.'

Gran settled in the armchair next to the Christmas tree. Merry was curled up on her lap, purring loudly. 'I'm so looking forward to the work being finished on the Centre, and planning next year.'

Lucy really did want to talk about the Centre with Gran, but first of all she wanted to talk about the little rabbit.

'Gran, I know the visitors haven't come yet—but would you mind if I slept downstairs tonight too so I can keep an eye on him?' said Lucy. 'I can sleep in the kitchen with Rocky and Scruffy. I can't sleep upstairs knowing that he is downstairs all alone, with no friends.'

'I think that's a lovely idea,' said Gran, smiling at her.

It was fun getting ready to sleep in the kitchen. Dad agreed to bring Rocky down, and Lucy brought Scruffy down too.

'We're having a sleepover with a rabbit,' she whispered in his ear.

Mum and Dad brought the camp

bed down and made it very warm and cosy, and Mum even put a hot-water bottle in it. Merry kept on getting in everyone's way, hiding under the pillows and burrowing under the duvet to find the hot-water bottle.

Lucy went upstairs to kiss Gran goodnight.

'If only we could find the rabbit's family,' said Lucy. 'It seems so sad not to be with your family at Christmas.'

'I'll help you look after him, Lucy,' said Gran. 'We might have to take him over to the wildlife sanctuary and see if we can gradually introduce him to a new warren in a safe area. It's not easy. It takes a lot of time, and the wild rabbits have to be allowed to come and sniff him through the wire fence so that they accept him.'

'What if they don't accept him?' said Lucy.

'Well, then we'd have to keep him in the Centre because it would be too dangerous for him on his own.'

'Come on, Lucy,' called Mum. 'Time for bed! Kiss Gran goodnight and come downstairs.'

Mum had brought in a coffee table and a little reading lamp, and Lucy put her snow globe on the table beside her.

'Goodnight, Lucy. Sleep well,' said

Mum, and she gave Lucy a hug. 'Have some hot chocolate and read a little bit of your book, and then go and brush your teeth. We'll come and kiss you goodnight on our way to bed.'

The kitchen seemed different after bedtime. Mum switched off the lights but left the one over the cooker on. Lucy had to remind herself that the shadows on the back of the door were only Mum and Dad's aprons hanging on the peg, the dark shapes in the corner were only Oscar's football boots, and the shapes coming down from the ceiling were only the pots and pans hanging from the rack. Outside the kitchen window, the garden seemed dark and mysterious. Inside, the fridge shivered and the ticking of the kitchen clock sounded much louder than during the day, but with Merry and Scruffy and Rocky, Lucy felt fine. It was a fun adventure to be sleeping somewhere new with friends—even if it was just the kitchen!

'Don't be frightened,' she called over softly to the sleeping rabbit. 'If you wake in the night, we're all here with you.'

Lucy finished her hot chocolate and went upstairs to the bathroom.

On her way back downstairs from brushing her teeth, Lucy heard Mum and Dad talking in the sitting room.

'I'm not sure if I can cope with a sick rabbit as well as Christmas for four more people,' said Mum.

'Don't worry,' said Dad. 'Lucy and I will take it to the sanctuary tomorrow.'

'It isn't fair,' said Lucy crossly as she got into bed. Merry was already curled up next to Scruffy on top of the duvet. Lucy looked over at Rocky and then at the cage. 'I hope he is going to be all right,' she said. The little rabbit stirred.

Lucy switched her reading lamp off but switched the snow globe on so that it lit up. She picked it up and shook the globe so the snow fell on the cottage inside.

'I wish you were a magic snow globe,' said Lucy. 'I'd close my eyes like this . . .' She closed her eyes as tight as she could and felt the cool globe in her hands. '. . . And I'd say, "I wish for that little rabbit to get better; I wish he could be back with his family for Christmas; and I wish for Christmas to be like it always is." '

All at once, Lucy felt her hands tingle. She opened her eyes quickly and saw that the globe was glowing brighter and brighter, the sparkling silver and white snowflakes falling faster and faster, even though she wasn't shaking the globe any more. Suddenly, Lucy was sure that beyond the twirling snowflakes she could see a tiny figure of Father Christmas outside the little house in the woods. He was waving to her and holding a sweet baby reindeer in his arms. At the same time, she heard the sound of sleigh bells and the globe felt warm in her hands. Then the whirling white and silver snowflakes were joined by first green and then red ones, and then all the snowflakes became tiny glittering stars of all the colours of the rainbow, filling the globe.

'You ARE a magic snow globe!' said Lucy in delight. Her heart beat fast with excitement and she felt a wave of

happiness from the top of her head to the tips of her toes.

Lucy blinked hard and shook her head, but when she looked back there was no snow falling, no rainbow stars, no Father Christmas, or baby reindeer. The tingling stopped and the snow globe felt cool as she held it. Everything was back to normal—it was just a pretty snow globe with a tiny house in a still wood with snow lying peacefully on the ground—but inside Lucy still felt fizzy with happiness.

'What just happened?' said Lucy out loud to Rocky, Merry, and Scruffy. 'Did I dream that?' Merry gave a little mew. She put her paws on Lucy's chest and climbed up, touching her little pink nose to Lucy's and looking into Lucy's eyes. Then she jumped onto Lucy's pillow and curled herself up, purring so much that Lucy could feel the vibrations.

'Merry! I don't speak "purr"! And you're so loud!' laughed Lucy. 'How am I going to sleep if you purr like that? I still don't know if the globe is really magic or if I only dreamt it. But I'm suddenly so, so tired. I think I'll just lie down next to you and . . .'

When Lucy's parents tiptoed in, only the light above the cooker and the light from the snow globe were on. Lucy was fast asleep, holding Scruffy, with Merry beside her and Rocky standing guard. They kissed her goodnight, and, as they closed the door and Lucy and Merry and the little rabbit stirred and slept, the pretty silver and white snowflakes inside the globe began to fall again, even though Lucy had not shaken it.

Chapter Four

22nd December

The rabbit was still sleeping when Lucy woke the next morning to the sound of Dad filling the kettle and whistling Christmas carols. Merry was also asleep on the pillow next to her. Lucy stroked her and she stretched and purred but didn't wake up. The snow globe was on the table. No snow was falling. It all looked completely normal.

'It must have all been just a lovely dream,' said Lucy, giving Scruffy a hug.

Lucy got out of bed and put on her dressing gown and slippers. First she went to check on the rabbit, but he didn't want to eat any of the food she tried to give him. He just lay with his eyes closed, his soft furry body going up and down with his breathing.

'Morning, Lucy Lu!' said Dad, giving her a kiss. 'I'm going to take your gran and your mum a cup of tea in bed. Do you want to help me?'

Lucy carefully carried a cup up to Gran.

'Thank you, Lucy,' said Gran. 'How is the rabbit?'

'He's not really eating yet,' said Lucy. 'He's sleeping.'

Gran took a sip of her tea. 'Poor little chap. Maybe he needs some more rest. It must have been a shock for him. I've got to do what the doctor said and have a little rest this morning too, but I'll come down later and we'll check him out. Don't worry.'

'Now, Lucy, I'll fold up the bed,' said Dad, when Lucy came back down to the kitchen. 'Please can you put the coffee table and the lamp away?'

Lucy slipped the snow globe into her pocket and carried the little table and the lamp back into the sitting room. Dad had switched on the fairy lights already and it looked warm and cheery.

'Well done, Lucy!' said Dad when she returned to the kitchen. 'I'll put the pillows and duvet in a bag in this cupboard, ready for tonight.'

Lucy walked over to check on the tiny rabbit. He looked back at her, his eyes open and his nose twitching, but he wasn't interested in the food in his cage. His fur looked so soft and brown, she longed to pick him up and give him a hug, but she knew from Gran that wild animals don't enjoy being cuddled.

She put her hand in her pocket and felt the smooth roundness of the snow globe. 'I wished you'd be better and home for Christmas,' she whispered to the rabbit. She checked Dad wasn't looking—he was busy making room in the cupboard for the bedding—and took the snow globe out quickly. But it looked just like it always did—not magic in the least. She must have imagined it after all. Lucy felt a little disappointed.

She had so wanted to help the rabbit.

'Lucy—what's this?' asked Dad. 'I found it under your pillow.' He gave Lucy a little red cloth pouch as he took the folded-up bed out to the garage.

Lucy had never seen the red pouch before. It was as red as Father Christmas's coat, and it sparkled as Lucy held it. It was so beautiful, embroidered with a picture of Father Christmas and a little white Christmas reindeer. Lucy opened the pouch, and inside was glittering, magical dust—all the colours of the rainbow, just like the stars she had seen in the globe. Folded up small and covered in glitter was a note. Lucy felt her heart beating fast. Her fingers were tingling the way they had felt when she had wished on the snow globe—something magical was happening, she was sure of it. She opened the note and read:

To Lucy.

This magic dust is especially for you
For with your kind heart you will
know what to do.
So sprinkle it carefully down from
above
on those who are lost and need
friendship and love
And magic will happen for them
and for you
And your christmas wishes
will then all come true.

What could it mean? Lucy was puzzling over the note when Oscar came rushing into the kitchen. Lucy hastily put the note in her pocket.

'I'm late to meet Will and Fergus,' he said, picking up his football boots from the corner.

'I need you to come back and clear your room later, Oscar,' said Dad, coming back into the room. 'We're going to have to put some luggage in there.'

'But Dad—what about my drums and all my other stuff?' complained Oscar. He looked at the clock. 'OK, I'll do it later. I'm late! I'll be back for lunch!' and suddenly he was off, banging the door behind him.

'Hmm. I'll have to make sure he remembers,' said Dad. 'Right,' he said to Lucy. 'I've just put some washing in the machine. Your mum and I have to go and do some more Christmas shopping this morning. Our visitors should be arriving tonight. Will you be OK staying here downstairs on your own this morning? I think we should let Gran have a sleep.'

'That's fine, Dad!' said Lucy, trying not to look too excited. She couldn't wait until everyone had gone so she could look at the magic note again. She felt bubbly with happiness. Something amazing was happening, and she wanted to look at the note and the magic dust properly when nobody else was there.

Chapter Five

When her mum and dad had gone
out, Lucy quickly got dressed. She
felt so excited about the pouch. Merry
made a bit of a fuss mewing for her
breakfast, winding in and out of Lucy's
legs, so Lucy fed her and then Merry

disappeared through the cat flap.

Lucy quickly put her pyjamas back inside Scruffy so that he looked lovely and plump again. She put him on top of Rocky in the corner of the kitchen. 'I suppose you eat pyjamas for breakfast,' she said to Scruffy, as she poured some Krispies into her bowl and added the milk. Normally she loved to listen to the rice pop, but today she was too busy reading and rereading the note to pay much attention. The paper itself glowed and sparkled as if it was trying to help her understand the words.

Suddenly, the telephone rang. Maybe it was Mum or Dad checking on her, or asking what she would like for tea?

'Hello?' said Lucy.

'Hello, Lucy!' said a man's friendly voice. 'This is your dad's friend, Prajit. We managed to get an earlier flight and so we'll be with you in about five minutes. Is your dad there?'

'No,' said Lucy. 'He'll be back soon.'

'I'll ring him on his mobile then,' said Prajit. He had an Australian accent and sounded kind. 'We'll see you very soon! Bye!'

Lucy put the phone down.

'Oh no!' she said to Rocky and Scruffy. 'The visitors are coming any minute!'

She ran over to check on the rabbit, but he was still asleep. She put the note back in the red pouch with the glitter, and carefully put it in her pocket. Then she washed up her cereal bowl and spoon, and put the cereal box back in the cupboard so that the kitchen table was tidy.

She heard the key turn in the door, and her mum and dad rushed back in.

'We've just spoken to Prajit so we came straight back!' said Mum. 'The rooms aren't ready! What shall we do?'

At that moment the doorbell rang and the house was full of cheery voices and laughter and people hugging.

Prajit and his wife Joanna were really friendly, and as soon as Mum saw them, she relaxed and started smiling. Sita, their daughter, was smaller than Lucy expected. She had big brown eyes like her dad and long dark hair. She was wearing a pretty blue velvet hairband with her name on it in silver. Lucy thought it was lovely. Sita wasn't smiley like her mum and dad. She hid behind her mum and wouldn't even look at Lucy.

'It's so lovely of you to have us for Christmas whilst we wait for the house to be ready!' said Joanna. 'We're so sorry to land ourselves on you like this.'

She handed Mum some parcels. 'We've brought some Christmas presents from Australia for you!'

At lunchtime, Dad went into the kitchen with Prajit to put the pizzas in the oven and catch up with his friend's news. Joanna and Sita stayed in the sitting room with Mum and Lucy. Oscar came back and went up to his room to get changed out of his football gear.

'Don't be silly, Sita. Say hello to Lucy,' said Joanna, but Sita just shook her head and looked down.

'I'm sorry, Lucy,' said Joanna. 'Sita's a bit tired from a long flight and she is missing her friends.'

'I'll just go and ask Gran if she wants any pizza,' said Lucy. She didn't want to have to stay in the sitting room with everyone, and especially Sita, who didn't seem to like her at all.

'Good girl!' said Mum. 'I'm sure she'll want to come down and join us.'

As Lucy went up the stairs, she could hear Joanna saying how lovely the Christmas decorations were and how exciting it would be if it snowed when they were in England. Sita didn't say anything at all.

Chapter Six

Gran came down, and everyone was very cheerful at lunch apart from Sita, who kept very quiet and wouldn't look at anyone.

'We need to pop into town to get some surprises,' said Joanna. 'We thought we'd do it before our journey catches up on us and we have to go to sleep. Is it OK if we leave Sita here with you?'

'Of course!' said Mum. 'Lucy and I were going to do our Christmas baking—it will be lovely to have her with us, won't it, Lucy?'

Lucy nodded, but she didn't want to say 'yes' out loud as it wasn't really true. She liked her special Christmas baking time with just her and Mum.

'That's lovely. Sita loves baking, don't you?' said Joanna, but Sita just put her arms around her mum and hid her head.

'Can I join in with the baking?' said Gran, which made Lucy feel a bit better.

'What about Oscar? Isn't he doing any baking? Come on—you can't just leave it to the girls!' said Prajit.

'And me? I think I'll do some too this year!' said Dad, looking over at Sita and giving her a wink. 'Perhaps Sita can give me some tips!'

After lunch, Joanna and Prajit went off to do their shopping. They said they would pick up the last bits of Christmas food Mum and Dad hadn't managed to get. Dad made Oscar stay and bake with everybody else. Oscar was a bit grumpy at first, and the kitchen felt a bit crowded, but Dad put on loud Christmas songs and gave everyone silly Christmas hats to wear. Lucy put hers on and went over to the side to see the rabbit. He had his eyes closed and was breathing heavily. He wasn't well.

'I'm sorry it's a bit noisy. It must be so awful feeling lost and ill away from your friends in the warren,' she whispered. Then she remembered:

. . . sprinkle it carefully down from above
On those who are lost and need friendship
and love . . .

'I think I know what to do!' Lucy said to herself. She checked nobody was watching and took the pouch out.

She nearly dropped it in surprise—the little figures of Father Christmas and the reindeer seemed to be moving! They looked like the figures she had seen in the snow globe. Father Christmas waved at her and the reindeer ran around in a circle.

They're telling me I've got it right! thought Lucy excitedly. *I've got to sprinkle it on the rabbit.*

'Come on, Lucy!' called Dad. 'We've got to make the cake mixture!'

'I'll be back as soon as I can,' whispered Lucy to the rabbit.

Although Lucy was impatient to be alone with the rabbit and use the magic dust, it was still fun cooking with Dad. Even Sita smiled a little when Dad showed everyone how to crack eggs and do a silly dance at the same time. Mum told him to stop but she kept laughing. They all did a silly dance around the kitchen, and then Dad asked Sita to show him how to put the cake mixture into the cases, and kept making deliberate mistakes to make her laugh.

Lucy beamed with excitement. She couldn't wait to see if she was right about the note. Dad saw her and laughed, and gave her a hug.

'We're going to have a great Christmas—I can feel it!' he said.

I know it, thought Lucy, touching the soft magical pouch in her pocket.

As soon as the cakes were in the oven and the others had all gone into the sitting room, Lucy took out the pouch.

'I think this dust might make you feel better,' she whispered to the rabbit. 'I made a wish on my snow globe and then this pouch arrived, so it must be magical,' and she quickly sprinkled some of the sparkling dust over the cage.

Lucy gasped as the wonderful sparkling dust didn't fall on the cage floor, but instead rose up in the air in a beautiful glittering rainbow cloud and whirled round and round the little rabbit. His eyes opened and he looked straight into hers. Lucy felt in her heart how much he wanted to go home, but she also felt certain that, somehow, the magic dust would help him.

'Everything is going to be all right—I just know it,' she whispered to him. He wriggled his nose and the magic dust disappeared, but Lucy felt sure everything was going to be fine.

'Hey! Look at the rabbit!' said Oscar, coming back into the kitchen. 'Look, everyone!' The others followed him and joined Lucy in the kitchen. They all stood together and looked over to the rabbit's cage. He was hopping about slowly, eyes wide open, nose twitching.

'The magic dust worked! Thank you, magic snow globe!' said Lucy under her breath.

'That's so good to see!' said Mum. 'He's obviously feeling a bit better. We must phone the sanctuary and ask when we can bring him over today. I'll do it now.'

'But the sanctuary is miles away. He will never get back to his own warren if we send him there,' said Lucy quickly.

'Lucy, dear,' said Gran. 'Remember—you can't just put a wild rabbit down a strange burrow and expect the other rabbits to welcome it. It takes weeks if you want to introduce a rabbit to a new warren. You have to keep it in a run in the middle of a safe field and let the wild rabbits come up and sniff it every night.'

'But what if it isn't a new warren, Gran? What if you KNOW where he comes from?'

'And do you?' said Gran.

'Not yet, but I think I can find out,' said Lucy. 'I really do, Gran.'

'Oh, Lucy,' said Gran. 'You're such a kind girl. That rabbit is lucky to have you. Look—why don't we keep him here another night? Maybe tomorrow we can find a field nearby—I could ask my friend who has helped me reintroduce rabbits before. But we do have to be careful, and we can't do anything like that if his leg is still poorly.'

'Thanks, Gran! Just let me have another night and I will try to find out where he is from.'

'How are you going to find that out, Lucy?' laughed Gran.

'I've got an idea!' said Lucy, her eyes sparkling with excitement.

Chapter Seven

Joanna and Prajit came back from shopping with lots of goodies. Delicious smells of baking drifted in from the kitchen, and when the timer went, Dad took the cakes out and put them on the cooling rack, and popped some jacket potatoes in for the evening meal.

As Gran was feeling so much better, they all got into partners and played cards around the table. It was a big squash and they had to pull up lots of chairs and beanbags, but they managed it, and Prajit and Joanna taught them a card game Lucy's family didn't know.

'I'll be Sita's partner, shall I?' said Gran, smiling at Sita so kindly that Sita smiled back. Lucy felt a bit cross. She wanted to be Gran's partner.

'I want Lucky Lucy!' said Prajit, sitting next to her, which made her smile.

'Well, I'll have Omazing Oscar!'

said Joanna, and everyone laughed, though Oscar went a bit red.

'That just leaves me and you together,' said Mum to Dad, who pulled a silly face. Sita giggled.

'Don't worry—you're my favourite!' said Mum, giving him a kiss, and Dad pretended to go weak at the knees.

Prajit was so good at the card game that he and Lucy won, though Oscar and Joanna kept saying they were cheating. Merry came in halfway through the game. Her fur was very cold and she wound in and out of everyone's legs, purring and asking to be stroked. Joanna and Prajit and Sita all made a big fuss of her.

'She's lovely! I wish I had a cat. You're so lucky, Lucy,' Sita said shyly.

Lucy felt very proud that Merry climbed up on her lap and fell asleep.

Before they knew it, it was dinner time. They cleared the cards away and all sat around the table eating lovely hot jacket potatoes. There were lots of different fillings to choose from. Lucy had beans and cheese in hers; Sita had pineapple and cheese. Mum put out the special Christmas candles with the angels' chimes. The angels spun round in the hot air rising from the candles, and hit against the bells, making a lovely tinkling sound. It all sounded so Christmassy.

'Let's ice the cakes now,' said Mum.

'Good idea!' said Dad. 'I'll make some icing and bring in the glittery balls and toppings and we can each do our own design.'

It was a lot of fun. Dad found some icing pens and wrote 'Dad' on his, but then Prajit wrote 'No. 1 Dad' on his in even bigger letters. Mum made a snowman's smiley face, and Joanna made a Christmas tree. Oscar used up

loads of silver balls to make an 'O' on
his. Lucy decided to ice a picture of a
little rabbit, and when she looked over,
she was surprised to see Sita had done
the same. Sita smiled shyly at her. It was

a lovely smile and Lucy smiled back.

They had their tea and cakes by the fire in the sitting room, Merry on Gran's lap, the coloured lights on the Christmas tree twinkling. First Sita yawned, then Prajit, then Joanna.

'Oh dear—excuse us!' laughed Joanna. 'It's been such a lovely day, but I suddenly feel so tired. I think we'd better go to bed!'

'I'll just come up to make sure you have everything you need,' said Mum.

'I'll set up camp in the kitchen for the girls,' said Dad.

Lucy looked over to where she had put the snow globe on the mantelpiece.

A few snowflakes were drifting down even though nobody had shaken it. Another secret message! Lucy felt so excited she could hardly bear the wait for everyone to go to sleep so she could carry out her plan.

'Come on, Lucy, let's get Sita's bed ready,' said Dad. 'The poor girl looks half asleep already.'

So they set up two camp beds in the kitchen, Merry getting in the way again.

'I'll pop her outside if she is bothering you, shall I?' said Dad.

'No—I don't mind her,' said Sita. 'She's so sweet.' Lucy was glad. She brought the snow globe in from the sitting room and put it beside her bed.

As soon as Sita was asleep, Lucy crept over to the rabbit. There was no way to check his leg but his coat seemed shinier and his breathing had calmed down too. The kitchen was dark except for the light from the snow globe, but as Lucy pulled the pouch out of her pocket, it glowed a soft red colour in the night. When Lucy opened the pouch, the dust inside twinkled and shone like lots of beautiful tiny jewels. It was magical.

'The note said that ALL my wishes would come true, so this dust that the magic snow globe has sent me must be able to help me return you to your warren,' she said.

Lucy sprinkled the dust over the cage. It fell in a sparkling rainbow down through the bars of the cage and onto the rabbit's fur. 'I wish I knew which warren you came from,' Lucy whispered. She gasped as the rabbit opened his eyes and looked into Lucy's. His fur glittered with the magic dust, while his eyes seemed to get wider and shinier. Lucy gazed straight at him and something truly magical began to happen.

Chapter Eight

As Lucy looked into the little rabbit's eyes, the kitchen, the camp beds, and even the rabbit seemed to disappear, and all she could see was a winter field in the moonlight with lots of rabbits running around playing, nibbling the grass, and hopping around a big oak tree. There were no clouds in the sky, but lots of stars. It was beautiful. Lucy recognized the tree—she played there with Rosie sometimes. Lucy could feel how happy and free the rabbits were together. Lucy was seeing the world through the eyes of the tiny rabbit!

Suddenly, a shadow fell across the field. It was the shadow of a big bird, hovering high up in the night sky above them, and it scared all the little rabbits. They scattered into their burrows, their tails white in the dark. Lucy's little rabbit got separated from the others and, instead of running down a burrow, he decided to run across the field to get away from the bird. He ran and ran, and Lucy could feel how frightened he was. She saw how he caught his foot on some wire as he pushed himself under a fence, and came to a busy road. In the night, the cars and the lorries were huge and noisy and their headlights dazzled the little rabbit. He was so scared of the bird, he ran across the road anyway. The cars screeched their brakes and Lucy saw the little rabbit run into an empty playing field and under a hedge, where he lay panting and all alone, as the big bird turned in the sky and flew away.

Then the pictures disappeared and Lucy was back in the kitchen, looking into the bright and shining eyes of the little rabbit. She could feel how much he longed to be back with his rabbit family in the warren.

'You poor thing,' whispered Lucy. 'You must have been so scared. And now you are far away from your friends and family. Don't worry. Thanks to the magic dust my snow globe sent me, I know exactly where your warren is. The big oak tree isn't far from here, and I'll get you home for Christmas, I promise.'

The little rabbit wiggled his nose, and Lucy knew he had heard and understood her. He lay down and closed his eyes.

Lucy sat on her bed. What could she do now? She knew EXACTLY where the little rabbit came from, but how was she going to keep her promise and get him home? Lucy crawled back into bed, determined to think of a way. It had been such a magical day. She rubbed her eyes with her hands, getting some of the glitter on her face. She looked over at Sita, sleeping peacefully. 'You've hardly said a word all day,' whispered Lucy. 'If only I knew what you were thinking.' Just then, something very strange happened. Lots of glittering rainbow colours swirled around in the air, just like the ones she had seen around the little rabbit, and instead of Sita quiet and asleep in her camp bed, Lucy could suddenly picture her laughing and playing with friends on a beach in the sun. It looked like lots of fun. There was a barbecue and Sita and her friends were running around throwing a ball. Then Lucy could see Prajit, Joanna, and Sita at a table in a house, and Sita was crying, even though her mum and dad were putting their arms around her and pointing to a calendar. Then she saw Sita and Prajit and Joanna walking up some steps to board a big plane, and lastly, Sita sitting by a window on the plane, looking out at the clouds and crying. Lucy could feel how sad and lonely she felt. Then the pictures faded.

Lucy looked down at her hands.

There was still some magic dust on them.

'Poor Sita. She feels the same way the rabbit does!' said Lucy to herself. 'Sita is sad and quiet because she misses her friends back home. I can't bring her back to Australia, but perhaps I can be her friend whilst she is here.' She looked over at Rocky in the corner. She couldn't see his kind eyes but he seemed to give a little rock as if to say, 'That's right, Lucy!'

It made Lucy feel good inside to think about helping the rabbit and Sita.

'My first two wishes came true, but I can't see how Christmas could possibly be like it used to be.' There was a tiny bit of dust in the bottom of the pouch and she turned it upside down so a few sparkling specks fell on Sita as she slept.

'I hope the magic dust gives you nice dreams,' said Lucy, and lay down in bed. 'Tomorrow will be great!' she whispered to Scruffy and Merry, and she quickly fell fast asleep cuddling them.

23rd December

'Rise and shine, sleepyheads!' came Dad's voice. 'You've slept half the morning!'

Lucy sat up with a start. The kitchen

was full of light and Dad was peeling potatoes at the sink.

'Good morning, Lucy and Sita!' said Mum, smiling down at them. 'You both slept so soundly nobody wanted to wake you, so we had breakfast in the sitting room. Oscar's off out with his friends again, and Sita's mum and dad are at the shops.'

Lucy got out of bed and rushed over to the rabbit. He was sitting up and immediately came over to the bars to sniff Lucy's hand.

'Look, Mum! Look, Sita! His leg is completely better!' said Lucy happily. 'You can't even see where it was cut now!'

Lucy gave Sita an especially big smile, as she remembered what the magic dust had shown her, and Sita smiled back and came over to join Lucy at the cage.

'Hello, bub!' said Sita softly. The little rabbit hopped over to her.

'What does that mean?' said Lucy.

'Oh, it's what we call a baby in Australia,' said Sita.

'That's what we'll call him then!' said Lucy, and they laughed. Lucy felt really good inside to see Sita looking happier.

They had boiled eggs and toast cut up into soldiers for breakfast, and

Sita taught Lucy to say more Australian words in an Australian accent, which was lots of fun.

'G'day, Gran!' said Lucy when Gran came into the room, and she and Sita got the giggles.

'Well hello, Lucy and Sita!' said Gran. 'I didn't realize you'd been to Australia overnight, Lucy!'

Lucy thought about how, in a way, she had, but she didn't say anything.

'My, that rabbit looks amazing!' said Gran. 'I can't believe it! I've never seen a leg heal like that. Perhaps it wasn't as bad as we thought. I didn't get a chance to look closely at it yesterday. You've done a wonderful job, Lucy. Sita dear, I wonder if you could come upstairs and help me with something. Maybe Lucy could help put away the beds and then join us after a bit?'

Sita went off with Gran. Lucy slipped the magic snow globe and the pouch into her dressing-gown pocket and cleared the table. Then Mum helped her fold up the beds and put them into the garage. As soon as everything was tidied away, Lucy rushed upstairs to join Gran and Sita, pushing open the door without knocking.

'Honestly, Lucy!' said Gran, putting something behind her back. 'You really should knock before you come into a room!'

Sita turned her back and was busy putting something into a bag.

'Sorry, Gran,' said Lucy.

'That's all right, but Sita and I have something private we are doing, just the two of us, you see,' said Gran.

Lucy felt a bit hurt.

'Come back later, Lucy,' said Gran. 'Actually, we'll come and get you. Close the door behind you, there's a good girl.'

Everything was going wrong. Why was Gran being so strange?

Lucy had one hand in her pocket as she sadly went downstairs again. She took the pouch out. There was no dust left inside and it just looked like a very pretty purse. There were no wishes left.

'Maybe I can wish on the snow globe again?' she said to herself—but the snow globe looked just as it always was, and stayed cool in her hands.

So is that the end of the magic? she wondered. But as she thought that, she heard a tinkling sound, like distant bells, and little bubbles of happiness started rising inside her, driving the sadness away. She didn't know why, but she felt sure that something wonderful was just around the corner.

Chapter Nine

'I can't get over how cold it is!' said Joanna, as Lucy came into the kitchen. 'The man in the corner shop said it might even snow. How perfect! Sita has never seen snow.'

'I'd better save a carrot and we can

make a snowman in the garden if it does,' said Dad.

'A snowman! I'd really like to make one!' said Sita, coming into the kitchen with Gran.

'It's great to see you've cheered up,' said Prajit, giving her a hug. 'I was getting a bit worried about you, but ever since you woke up this morning you seem back to your old self!'

Sita smiled at Lucy, and the little bit of jealousy Lucy felt about Gran spending time with Sita disappeared. Everything was going to be fine, she could feel it.

'Who is coming to see Oscar and his

friends play football?' said Mum. 'They have a Christmas five-a-side today up at the park. We can go before lunch.'

'I'm coming!' said Gran. 'I feel so well and I'd really like a little walk and a chat with Lucy on the way,' and she took Lucy's hand. Lucy beamed.

Upstairs Lucy quickly got dressed. She took the snow globe out of her pocket and gave it a shake. The snowflakes just fell as normal, but Lucy remembered the rainbow stars she had seen, and what she had seen in the little rabbit's eyes.

'I've got to trust in the globe—it promised me my wishes would come true, it sent me the magic dust, and I know it showed me where Bub comes from,' Lucy decided. 'I'm going to ask Gran if I can take Bub back to the field with the oak tree tonight. I hope she agrees,' she said to herself.

'Come on, Lucy!' called Dad up the stairs. 'I don't want to miss Oscar score the winning goal!'

They all set out for the short walk to the park. The sky was a cold slate grey and Lucy was glad she had her hat, coat, scarf, and gloves on.

'I can't believe how well the rabbit

looks!' said Gran, as they walked along together. 'I was wondering if you could show me where you found him.'

'Gran! If I could tell you where his warren is, would it be too late to take him back? I think I know where it is, Gran!' said Lucy, swinging her gran's arm excitedly. 'Can I show you?'

'Well, Oscar and his friends don't seem to have started properly yet, so let's have a look,' said Gran.

Lucy took Gran and Sita to the hedge where she had found the rabbit, and then they crossed the road to another field with a big oak tree. Lucy tried to remember what the rabbit had showed her, and she looked for the bit of the fence he had squeezed under and caught his foot on.

'Look, Gran! Here is a little bit of fur. This is where Bub caught his foot— I am sure of it! I think he was running from a bird of prey. And look, Gran— look what is in the field!'

Gran looked over. 'Well,' she said, 'the fur on the fence is rabbit fur. It definitely looks like there is a warren there—look at all the entrances to the burrows! It would make sense that this is where he came from . . . If only we could be sure . . .'

'Gran, please can we bring Bub here

tonight when it is dusk and the rabbits come out? Please. I'm sure we will know for sure then,' said Lucy.

'Oh! Please can I come too?' said Sita excitedly. 'I'd really like to see little Bub go home!'

'Well, perhaps if your dad drives us here, Lucy, and your mum and dad agree you can come, Sita. But if I don't think we are doing the right thing, and it looks like the other rabbits are going to fight Bub, then we will bring him back home with us. All right, girls?' said Gran.

'All right,' said Lucy. She just had to hope that the magic snow globe would fix things.

They watched the football match. Will and Oscar scored a goal each and Fergus did a brilliant save so that in the end their team won and Oscar was very happy. Then they all came home for hot soup and rolls and lots of cheese, and in the afternoon they played Scrabble. Oscar made the words 'ball' and 'goal', and everyone laughed. Gran found the letters for 'bunny' and Lucy spelt 'home' and they smiled at each other.

'Could you drive Lucy and Sita and me up to the field across the road from the park tonight?' said Gran to Lucy's dad. 'We are going to have a little adventure and see if we can return the rabbit home. It looks like the nearest warren.'

'Oh, please can I go?' said Sita to her mum and dad. 'He's such a sweet rabbit. I'd like to see him back with his friends.'

Lucy remembered the magic pictures of Sita she had seen. Sita needed friends as much as the rabbit.

'What do you think?' said Gran. 'Can Sita come?'

'Please—I'd love Sita to come too!' said Lucy, and as she said it, she found that she meant it.

'Of course!' said Joanna and Prajit, smiling.

'Thank you!' said Sita, and the next word she made in Scrabble was 'friend'.

'Look!' she said to Lucy, and Lucy felt very happy. Sita was going to live in her village, and Lucy suddenly knew she would be a good friend. She couldn't wait for her to meet Rosie

Just as it was dusk, Dad drove them to the field with the rabbit in the cage.

Lucy could feel how hopeful and excited he was getting as they got nearer. His little nose was twitching, and his eyes were shining happily. She had the snow globe in her pocket and she held it tightly.

'Please make it all right for little Bub,' she wished.

They all got out of the car, and Lucy and Sita helped Dad and Gran carry the cage over the stile into the field. The evening mist was hanging in the air, and it all felt very still and magical as they walked across the field under the grey snow clouds. They could see lots of little white tails disappear into burrows as they walked nearer to the warren. The little rabbit was very alert, sitting up in the cage.

'What do we do now?' asked Dad.

'Well, we put the cage down and see what happens,' said Gran. 'We'll walk back to the car so the rabbits can't see us and we'll watch from there. The cage door is locked so he will be safe if they don't accept him.'

They put the cage down, and Lucy looked into the little rabbit's eyes. He was so sweet, and she knew she would miss him, but she could feel how excited and happy he was to be back in his field.

'Bye, Bub!' said Sita. 'Hope you find your friends!'

'Bye-bye, little rabbit,' whispered Lucy. 'Have a happy Christmas!'

Then they walked back to the car and turned back to look.

'My goodness!' said Gran. 'I've never seen anything like it!'

Chapter Ten

All around the cage were lots and lots of rabbits. The little rabbit was looking out at them and scrabbling at the cage as if he wanted to get out.

'Oh dear. I hope he won't hurt himself,' said Gran, 'I think we should go back.'

There was a little flash of sparkling rainbow colour over where the cage was.

'What was that?' said Dad, puzzled.

It's the last of the magic dust! Lucy thought happily. It's the final part of the wish coming true.

Then they saw the cage door fly open and the little rabbit run out!

'Oh no!' said Gran worriedly. 'I can't have locked it properly.' But soon she was smiling. The rabbits were nuzzling each other and hopping around, and the little rabbit was in the middle of the group, totally at home. He sat for a minute on his back legs and looked

in their direction as if to say thank you. Lucy made eye contact with him.

'Good luck, Bub!' she whispered, and she knew deep down that he had understood.

Then, with a flash of white tail, Bub and all the others disappeared back down into the burrows.

'Well, that was a big success!' said Dad. 'I thought it was much harder than that normally.'

'It is,' said Gran, looking puzzled. 'But I suppose it IS Christmas and everyone knows magical things happen at this time of year!' She reached over and gave Lucy and Sita a big hug. 'That little rabbit looked so well—you really have a special gift with animals, Lucy.'

Sita and Lucy sat in the back of the car with the empty rabbit cage wedged between them as they drove home.

'Bub was so lovely,' said Sita, 'but I'm glad he is back with his friends.'

'When my friend Rosie comes back from her Grandad's, you can meet her,' said Lucy. 'We'll all be in the same class at school. I know you miss your friends back in Australia, Sita, but can we be your friends whilst you are here?'

'I'd like that, Lucy!' said Sita. 'I think England will be fun.'

That night, Lucy and Sita played

with Lucy's Christmas puppet theatre before they went to bed. Sita loved the little baby reindeer figure. Lucy put the snow globe back next to her bed. It was as pretty as ever, but somehow it didn't look magical any more, and when Lucy touched it, there was no special tingly feeling.

Perhaps all the magic's used up now - and anyhow there's no more magic dust, thought Lucy. *But I'm glad not all my wishes came true. I wanted Christmas to be like it always is, but that didn't happen—and it's better! I love being friends with Sita—and I know Rosie will too. I'm so happy that wish WASN'T granted!*

Chapter Eleven

24th December

The next day was Christmas Eve, and
full of fun. Mum took Lucy to the
Christmas market and they bought
a tiny snow globe with a rabbit in for
Sita's Christmas present.

In the afternoon they all went off

into secret places around the house and wrapped presents, so that the pile of packages by the Christmas tree got higher and higher. Merry got far too excited and tried to climb it, so they had to put her in the kitchen with an early present—a special cat activity centre with tunnels and posts and toy mice hanging down on strings. Merry absolutely loved batting them with her paws.

At night they went off to church to hear Christmas carols by candlelight, and as they walked home, they felt something cold and light and feathery on their faces.

'Is it snow?' asked Sita.

'Yes!' said Lucy.

'I had such a lovely dream about it snowing at Christmas!' Sita said happily.

25th December

Christmas Day came, and everywhere was dusted with snow.

'How pretty!' said Sita, as she

woke up. 'I'm so glad to be here for Christmas!'

'I'm glad you're here too!' said Lucy.

They had a special breakfast of delicious pastries and croissants and some yummy Italian panettone cake. Then they all gathered around the Christmas tree to open their presents. Joanna and Prajit had brought some really fun things—Lucy and Oscar each had a boomerang, Mum had a brooch in the shape of a kangaroo, Gran had one in the shape of a koala, and Dad had a didgeridoo, a musical instrument like a decorated wooden drainpipe.

'I kept it hidden in the car boot as I thought you'd guess,' laughed Prajit. 'I'll teach you to play it!'

'Oh no! Prajit is the world's worst player!' groaned Joanna.

'Not now Dad has one!' said Oscar.

'Cheeky boy!' said Dad, 'I've had a go at one before—listen!' He blew into it and managed to make a very loud deep humming note from the instrument, which made little Merry jump and run behind a chair. She peeped out crossly until Lucy picked her up and gave her a cuddle.

'Thank you,' said Sita as she unwrapped her snow globe. 'It's lovely!'

'Lucy—this is from me,' Gran said, handing her a soft parcel. 'But before I give it to you, I want to make a special announcement!'

Everyone stopped talking and opening their presents to listen.

'As you know, I'm much better now that my shoulder has been fixed, so I have decided that I am going to open my Wildlife Rescue Centre again in the New Year. I don't think I will be able to do it on my own without an assistant, though, and after talking to your mum and dad, I would like it to be you, Lucy. You have a very special gift with animals, and I would like you to work with me during the holidays and when you have time at the weekends. This will explain your present.'

Lucy unwrapped it. Merry immediately jumped all over the paper as Lucy lifted out a very special red sweatshirt.

'Sita was very kind and helped me finish it off, as I couldn't sew as much as I wanted when I was in hospital. I'm sorry if we rushed you out of your room, but that's what we were hiding from you the other day,' said Gran. 'This is your uniform. There is the special Wildlife Rescue Centre logo on the front, and on the top of the sleeve, look what there is . . .'

Lucy looked, and saw it was a badge with a lovely embroidered rabbit.

'It's lovely!' she said.

'Every time you look after an animal I will embroider a new badge for you to put on your uniform, so everyone can see what a kind and clever animal lover you are!' said Gran, giving her a kiss.

Lucy beamed with pride. 'Thank you so much, Gran! I'd LOVE to be your assistant at the Centre! I can't think of anything better!'

That night, Lucy lay in her camp bed in the kitchen, cuddling Scruffy. Merry was asleep at her feet, and Sita was asleep in her bed, but Lucy lay awake, shaking the snow globe and thinking about what a lovely day they had had. She thought about Christmas dinner, with everyone crowded round trying to pull crackers and laughing, and Dad setting fire to the Christmas pudding, and how funny everyone looked in their hats. She thought about the snow rabbit that was in the garden. She and Sita had managed to make it after Christmas dinner, and the others had built a funny snowman next to it. Sita was definitely going to be a very special friend.

'I just wish I knew how our rabbit is,' she said to Scruffy and Rocky, and as she said it, the snow globe glowed one last time, and suddenly, Lucy saw her rabbit in the snow globe, looking up at her.

He looked so sweet and happy, as if he was smiling.

'Thank you,' she felt him say to her.

His little ears gave a twitch and he turned and disappeared. The globe showed her one last picture—a little pile of sleeping rabbits curled up cosy and warm together in a burrow. One raised his head and looked at her and she knew it was hers, and that he was safe and home.

'Thank you, magic snow globe, and goodnight, little Bub,' Lucy whispered, and with a sound of sleigh bells the picture inside the globe went back to being a pretty little house in a wood, with the snow falling. 'Happy Christmas!'

Thank you . . .

To the vet Rob McMeeking who talked to me about holding rabbits, and to Krista from The Wildlife Haven Rescue and Rehabilitation Centre for talking to me on the phone about rescuing rabbits.

To my lovely husband Graeme and my children Joanna, Michael, Laura and Christina.

To my agent Anne Clark, and Liz Cross and my editors Clare Whitston and Debbie Sims and all at OUP.

To Sophy Williams for her wonderful illustrations.

And a special hello to Rosie, who sent me a lovely card and drawing after reading Lucy's Secret Reindeer. I hope you notice your name is in this book!

About the author

Every Christmas, Anne used to ask for a dog. She had to wait many years, but now she has two dogs, called Timmy and Ben. Timmy is a big, gentle golden retriever who loves people and food and is scared of cats. Ben is a small brown and white cavalier King Charles spaniel who is a bit like a cat because he curls up in the warmest places and bosses Timmy about. He snuffles and snorts quite a lot and you can tell what he is feeling by the way he walks. He has a particularly pleased patter when he has stolen something he shouldn't have, which gives him away immediately. Anne also has two hens called Anastasia and Poppy. Anne lives in a village in Kent and is not afraid of spiders.

Make your own snow globe!

Do you want to make your own snow globe, just like Lucy's? We can't promise it will be magic, but it will look magical!

You will need an assistant, so make sure that an adult helps you

What you will need:

Clean jam jar

White plasticine

Plastic model trees and festive figures (Christmas cake decorations are perfect!)

Glitter

Water

Glycerin (available from chemists)

Epoxy resin glue, or any other waterproof glue (available from DIY and craft shops)

A helpful grown up to do some gluing

What to do

❄ Inside the lid of your jar build a snowy hill from the white plasticine. This will make it easier to see your little figures.

❄ Place the figures and trees on the hill.

❄ Ask an adult to glue the hill and figures in place for you, and leave to dry for 15 minutes.

❄ Fill the jar with water, almost to the very top. Add two teaspoons of glitter, two drops of glycerin, and stir.

❄ Screw the lid tightly back on to your jar. Make sure it is on properly, so it does not leak.

❄ Turn upside down, gently shake, and watch the snow swirl around!

A day in the life of a wildlife rescue worker

A rescue worker has a very busy job, especially in the spring and summer when there are lots of baby animals to care for. The day starts very early and there is often work to do in the middle of the night!

Morning

All the animals and birds that are in the rescue centre must be fed and their cages and pens cleaned. Some very young creatures need feeding many times during the day. Tiny birds may have to be fed every few minutes! There are lots of different sorts of foods to get ready and lots of food bowls to be washed.

The rescue worker may get called out to help an animal that is hurt. They will go in a wildlife ambulance and take special equipment. They may even need to take a boat. Sometimes they work with other rescue centres, the police or the fire brigade.

Afternoon

There are more animals to feed and lots of cleaning jobs to finish. New animals that have arrived will need special care. The worker may have to see a vet for special tests such as X-rays.

Lots of people phone the rescue centre and the rescue worker will spend time talking to people about how to help wild animals.

Evening

All the animals will be checked to see that they are warm and have food and water. Many animals will have to be given medicine to make them better. During the night, when most people are asleep, there is still work to do at a rescue centre. Some baby animals may need to be fed, and very poorly animals will need special care. The rescue worker can also be called out during the night to help animals that are hurt.

Then it's time for some sleep before another busy day !

The WILDLIFE HAVEN

What to do if you find an injured animal

If you find a wild animal or bird that you think is injured or poorly, find an adult to help. Wild animals are usually very frightened of people, so it is important that you keep as quiet as possible when you are near them. Do not let dogs and cats near the animal as this can scare them.

Advice for the "grown ups":

If you can get up close to a wild animal or bird it may be sick or injured. It is important to remember that most wild animals find human contact very stressful. Keep quiet and move slowly. Some wild animals will bite or scratch if they are frightened. Be aware of your own safety and contact an experienced wildlife rescue worker if dealing with species such as fox, badger, otter, deer or squirrel.

If you find a baby wild animal that appears to be orphaned, seek advice before touching it. Some species such as deer and hare leave their young for long periods of time. They hide and remain quiet until the mother returns to feed them. Baby animals that are blind with little or no fur should not be out alone. They will need to be picked up and kept warm until a rescue centre can be contacted.

Baby birds that have no feathers should not be out of the nest. If you are not able to locate the nest they will need to be kept warm until you can contact a rescue centre. Baby birds that have left the nest are called fledglings. They will have feathers and able to stand. They should be left alone unless they appear to be sick or injured.

Wildlife rescue centres can be located through the internet. Veterinary practices may also hold contact numbers. Some rescue centres are dedicated to one species of animal and there are also individuals that are registered to care for certain species such as hedgehogs and bats.

Thank you to **The Wildlife Haven Rescue and Rehabilitation Centre** for all of their help. Find out more about them at their website: **www.thewildlifehaven.co.uk**

If you enjoyed Lucy's Magic Snow
Globe then read on for a taster
of another of Lucy's festive
adventures,

Lucy's Secret Reindeer:

Lucy has a big secret . . . Santa's
left her a little reindeer in the
garden shed! Here's the moment
when she finds him:

'Hello, Starlight,' she whispered.
'Don't be frightened. It's Lucy.' She
tiptoed carefully forward, moving a
bucket to the side as she went. The
reindeer was only about the size of
Rocky—not much bigger than a small
dog. He was so little he didn't even

have big antlers like the pictures on Christmas cards; just baby ones, peeping through his fluffy coat.

How could you ever help to pull a sleigh? Lucy wondered. She had never been this close to a reindeer. She'd never even seen one in real life before. This was a real, live animal, not a picture or a toy. She put her hand out slowly and felt him reach out his soft muzzle to nudge it. Gran always told her never to rush an animal when you meet it. Starlight's breath was warm but his nose was cold. He was lying down on his side, his long legs splayed out. His big brown eyes had long eyelashes and he looked bewildered. He shivered a little.

'You're cold,' Lucy said anxiously, and edged herself forward so that she could sit cross-legged on some sacking next to him. When she felt ill the first thing her mum did was put her in bed and wrap her up so that she was cosy and warm. She looked around for something to wrap him up in. There was an old picnic rug they hadn't used since the summer, an old gardening jacket Dad used sometimes, and more sacking.

Starlight's tail wagged a little. It reminded Lucy of the lambs in the fields at springtime. She opened her coat and carefully pulled him up on to her knee, then she tried to snuggle them both under some sacking, Dad's jacket, and the rug. At first he was all long legs and baby antlers, and it was a bit tricky sorting out all the layers, but she knew she had to warm him up by cuddling him. Eventually he settled down on her lap. He was surprisingly light and furry, and just holding him in her arms made her think of stars and snowflakes and Christmas bells and the feeling you get when school finishes for the holidays.

'I wish I could take you into school to show everyone,' she said, stroking his soft fur. He sniffed and snuffled and gently nuzzled her face and looked deep into her eyes. Then he sighed, tucked his long legs up, and snuggled into her, his hard baby antler buds resting against her chest. It was a bit uncomfortable, but finally she managed to shuffle into a position against the wall. Soon the shed was full of the sound of a baby reindeer snoring.

'I can't believe you're here, Starlight,' she said, looking down at the sweetest little reindeer she could ever have imagined. 'But what should I do now?' Starlight just wriggled in his sleep, his ears twitching. He shivered again and Lucy held him tighter to keep him warm. She knew it was up to her to get him well for Christmas.

Here are some other stories we think you'll love!